THE CON

A SHORT STORY

VINEET VERMA

This story is a work of fiction. All the characters and events portrayed are fictitious. Similarities to real people, places, or events are coincidental.

Copyright 2025 Vineet Verma
Cover Design by James, GoOnWrite.com

All rights reserved. The distribution of this story without permission is a theft of the author's intellectual property. If you would like permission to use any material (other than for review purposes), please contact sayhello@vineetvermaauthor.com. Thank you for your support of the author's rights.

1

Elsa

Anyone paying any attention to Elsa Gardner could tell she was distressed. She jiggled the door of the white Toyota Camry parked on the street, checked her pockets and the ground around the car for the key, paced frantically and smacked her forehead with an *Oh no* before restarting the cycle by returning to the car door as if it might magically open. The panic in her voice amplified the effect, and the tears threatening to spill from her eyes at any moment cemented the image.

Her efforts were in vain. The door didn't budge. She didn't locate the key either. As she turned for another round of frantic pacing, she bumped into a man coming her way.

"Sorry, miss," he said.

She looked up at him, a river of hope surging inside her, and said, "No, *I'm* sorry. It's just that I—"

"What's the problem?" he asked, his face a picture of concern. "You look stressed. Anything I can do to help?"

"I ... I've locked myself out of my car, and I can't find the key. And I've got to be someplace in thirty minutes. It's very important," she replied as she ran her hand through her hair nervously.

He smiled in a manner intended to calm her nerves. "That sucks. I've been there before." A pause. "Can't you Uber it and figure out the car situation later?"

"Oh. I don't have Uber. Or Lyft. Or any of those apps."

"Really?" he asked, staring at her as if she'd landed from another planet.

"Yes. I just drive everywhere," she replied, suppressing the urge to imply that it was a dumb question. That would only antagonize him. "Besides, I feel those services exploit the drivers."

"Seems like you don't have much of a choice, then. I wish I could drop you, but I took the bus myself."

"Thank you." She flashed a grateful smile, wiping the tears from her eyes. "This is awkward, but ... do you have any cash?"

Doubt crept into his face, and he studied her for a bit. Elsa was confident that she was dressed well enough that the man wouldn't take her to be one of the numerous homeless begging for handouts.

"Cash?" he asked.

"For a cab."

"A cab," he replied, sounding skeptical.

She tried to remember the last time she'd seen a cab cruising the streets of San Jose. It was evident that the man had the same thought, because he asked, "And how are you going to find one?"

Elsa shrugged. "I don't know, but it's my best shot. I'll pay you back later. I promise."

He considered her response for a few moments before reaching into the back pocket of his jeans to produce his wallet. He flipped it open and surveyed the contents. A victorious grin followed as he fished out a twenty-dollar bill.

"This is all I've got." He held the note out to her.

She grabbed it before he had a chance to change his mind. "Thank you. Thank you. Thank you. You're a lifesaver."

"You're welcome. Glad I could help. Good luck with the cab."

And just like that, the man was off. *Not bad*, she thought as she stole a glance at the 7-Eleven at the corner. Satisfied with what she saw, she scanned the rest of the street and spotted a diner. Her stomach rumbled, sensing that relief was near. She headed towards the restaurant.

Rich aromas attacked her the moment she stepped inside. Her stomach growled again in anticipation. She slipped into an empty booth and beckoned the waitress. Bacon, scrambled eggs, toast, pancakes. She ordered it all. Fiscal prudence demanded that she save some of her new-found wealth, but if there was ever a time to be reckless, this was it. Her mouth flooded with saliva as she surveyed the rest of the diner, watching people stuffing themselves. They probably enjoyed the luxury three times a day, every day. *When was the last time she had eaten real food?* It seemed like an eternity. It was a miracle she hadn't collapsed already.

As she waited, she thought about the kind man — a simple, unsuspecting soul who had handed over the last of his cash to a stranger. He hadn't even taken her up on her offer to pay him back later. It was heartening to know that such people still existed, though it pained her to acknowledge that crooks like her were the reason a lot of people had stopped trusting their brethren.

Her thoughts were interrupted as the waitress placed her breakfast feast before her. Elsa thanked her and grabbed a bacon strip, wolfing it down in a second and repeating the trick with the next one. She had just picked up a forkful of egg when a man slid into the seat across the table. His ratty smile did nothing to diminish her appetite, and she stuffed her mouth and chewed carefully. Only once she had savored the egg to her satisfaction did she raise her eyebrow at this intrusion.

"Eddie," he said, extending his hand.

2

EDDIE

Eddie stepped out of the 7-Eleven, the five thousand dollars in cash in his pocket warming his body and soul. Or it would warm his soul if he hadn't already sold it to the devil. He chuckled at the thought.

Another successful scam. One more idiot parting with his hard-earned money thanks to his fear of the IRS. While Eddie enjoyed the long cons more, these quick scams provided easy income without as much planning. As he stood there with a goofy grin on his face, a woman walked over to a Camry parked on the street and peeked inside. A few furtive glances around, a peek at the parking meter. He was intrigued. She was beautiful and well-dressed — not the kind of woman who would nick a car, he would assume, but he was certain she was up to no good.

And then he saw it. Her act in all its glory. *Not bad*, he thought. For an amateur. He continued to watch as she played her part, finally walking away with the twenty bucks she had earned. There was potential there, he noted. Soon he was following her to the diner. He didn't enter at first, choosing to observe her through the glass to size her up before approaching.

Once he was satisfied, he entered and slid into her booth as if he belonged, as if he was meeting a friend, flashing his most charming smile to warm her up for his pitch. The way she had attacked those bacon strips, he knew she was starving. It was a feeling he was familiar with, the years of struggle still fresh in his memory. He hadn't expected her to continue eating on his arrival. He had anticipated shock, outrage. But she continued to chew on her eggs, only raising an eyebrow. A cool customer. He had judged her well, he thought. His plan might just work.

She ignored his extended hand. Having swallowed, she said, "Do you always violate strangers like this?" before continuing with her next forkful. Yes, he was certain now she hadn't eaten in days, given the laser focus on filling her belly.

"I'm sorry about this intrusion. But it's just that I saw what you did out there."

She froze. The color drained from her face. Of course, she must be worried he was going to arrest her for the crime she had just committed.

"Don't worry, you're not in any kind of trouble. The reason I'm here ... I'm in the same line of work."

He had expected her to be relieved, but, instead, confusion reigned on her face.

"What I'm trying to say is, I'm not a cop or anything. I'm a con man — a hustler, like you."

"Ah." She nodded. "What do you want from me? If you're looking for money, I just blew it on breakfast." She pointed to her emptying plate.

"Yeah, I noticed. Don't get me wrong, but that was a pretty amateurish con."

"It was?"

"Yes. All that effort for a measly twenty bucks. Doesn't that tell you something?"

"Bad luck. And it wasn't much trouble. Could easily have been a hundred bucks another time."

Eddie shook his head. "People don't carry a lot of cash around here. You're lucky you even got the twenty."

Elsa shrugged.

"And one more point. What would you have done if the real owner showed up?"

"I'd say it was a mistake. That my car looks the same. That I'd just remembered mine was parked on the next street."

Eddie smiled. "That would work."

"That's what you came here for? To tell me I messed up?"

"No. The thing is, I have a job."

"Well, good for you. You don't need to rub it in."

"No, no. You misunderstand. I'm planning a con, and I need help. That's where you come in."

"You want to hire me?"

Eddie nodded, his voice dropping to little more than a whisper. "Two million dollars."

Her eyes widened, as he'd expected they would. Then she burst out laughing. This, he hadn't expected.

"What's so funny?"

"You're pulling my leg, aren't you?"

"No. I'm serious. I don't waste time on sick jokes."

"So you're offering me two million dollars for this job?"

Eddie shook his head. "The take is two million. We split it seventy-thirty."

"I get the seventy?"

"No. I do."

He saw the wheels churning in her head as she worked out the math on what she could make. A fortune for someone struggling to make ends meet. It was a figure she would only have dreamed of. There was no way she was going to turn him down.

"What do I have to do?"

"There's this guy — Eric Abner. Rich dude. I hear he's got around two million in cash and gold bars sitting in his house."

"Hmm. And you're going to break in and steal it?"

"No. That would be impossible. He stores it in one of those high-end safes."

"You could always point a gun at him. Force him to open it."

"I don't do guns. Or knives. I'm a con man, not a violent criminal."

"So what's the plan, then?"

"You seduce him. Get—"

"I what?"

The look on her face told him he must be insane, and for a moment he believed it.

"Look. You're a beautiful woman. He's a young guy. You win his trust and get the combination. Then you can swipe the stuff any time."

The color rose in her face. Her intensity shook him. Maybe he'd erred by picking her.

"You want me to sleep with him for money? What does that make me?"

He hoped he could still salvage the situation. "It's not like that."

She raised an eyebrow. "It isn't?"

"So you won't do it?"

She was quiet, and silence reigned for an entire minute before she spoke again. Eddie waited, hating the fact that he was nervous, that he was worried she would decline his generous offer.

"I'm doing all the work. Why do I only get thirty percent?"

The nerve! he thought. "It's my idea. I'm the one who found this opportunity, the one who spent hours on research. If you don't like the terms, you can walk away. I'll find someone else."

In the silence that followed, he regretted letting his ego get the better of him. Perhaps he should not have been so harsh in his response. He should have left the door open for a negotiation.

"No, it's okay. Tell me more."

Eddie inwardly sighed in relief, thankful that she was as desperate as he had deduced.

"Not here. It's not safe. Meet me at my apartment tonight. I'll text you the address."

She hesitated, only for a second, and if not for his keen eye he would have missed it. But then she caved and shared her phone number. With everything settled, he walked away, excited about what was to come.

3

Elsa

A shudder had coursed through Elsa when Eddie invited her to his apartment. Was it what it sounded like? Another creepy man trying to take advantage of her, inviting her over to satiate his desires? She had hoped not, because the opportunity was too tempting to pass up. The last few months had been brutal, her run of bad luck continuing with force. Every con fell flat. Self-doubt had started creeping in. Having burnt through most of her savings, she was losing hope. Another month and she would be out on the streets. This con with Eddie could turn things around. She had decided she would take her chances.

By the time Elsa left her apartment that night, the hunger pangs had taken root again. She was thankful the breakfast had lasted her this long, but she was disappointed it wouldn't get her through the evening. She walked towards Eddie's apartment, which was only a couple of miles away. Not that she could have afforded any form of transport even if he'd lived further. Her beat-up Civic was low on gas, and she dared not let that level drop any lower. The little purse she clutched contained a can of pepper spray, in case Eddie tried any funny business. A spritz of the can in his eyes and a kick in the nuts would do the trick, she figured. It had worked with others in the past.

Yet, her heart raced as she knocked on his door. It didn't take long for him to open it. Strains of Miles Davis hit her ears as he stood there, a glass of what looked like whiskey in his hand. His lips parted in a wide grin.

"Come in," he said.

She followed, her hand inside her purse now, gripping the can tight. It was a studio apartment, cleaner and better furnished than she had expected. She started when she heard the front door shut, and she turned around to face him.

"Care for a drink?" Eddie asked.

She shook her head. It was critical that she stay alert for this meeting. Besides, it was possible he would drug her to make her more pliant. That's if sex was what he was after.

"Pizza?" he asked.

The sight of the box, three slices of pepperoni pizza staring at her invitingly, exacerbated her hunger. It was tempting to say yes, but she demurred.

"No, thanks," she replied.

"Well, more for me, then," he said as he grabbed a slice and took a big bite. He motioned to her to sit on the couch as he chewed. "Oh, this is so good," he said as he ingested another mouthful.

Elsa watched, bursting with temptation. She salivated, imagining what it would be like to taste some of that doughy goodness, to fill her insistent belly. But she ignored the thoughts and tried to focus on the task at hand. There would be a lot more pizza in her life once she pulled off this job. *If* she did, she reminded herself.

"So, about this con. Eric Abner," she asked, refusing to waste any more time. Not wanting to spend a moment more than necessary with Eddie.

"Oh, yeah. Abner. So, he's an up-and-coming real estate hotshot. Worth a few million already. Like I told you earlier, word is, he keeps some of his millions at home."

Elsa's hopes dipped. "You said *word is*. So this is just what you've heard in passing? You aren't sure about it?"

Eddie winced. "Lady, we wouldn't be here if I wasn't a hundred percent sure. This comes from a reliable source."

"So why doesn't this source steal it himself?"

"Because it's not so easy. It's not like Abner's laid it out on a table and you stroll in and rake in the money. He's got it in a secure safe somewhere in the house. Only he knows where it is, and only he knows the combination, of course." Eddie paused to grab another slice. "And that's where you come in." He pointed the slice at her. "You get cozy enough with him and he's bound to slip up sometime and open it in front of you. Guys like him won't miss an opportunity to impress a gal like you. To show you they're loaded."

Elsa bristled at the *gal like you* comment. What was he implying?

"But what if he doesn't?"

"He will. Trust me. If you keep him happy, do the stuff he likes — you know what I mean." Eddie's face lit up in a mischievous grin.

Slap him. Hard. Wipe that grin off his face, a voice inside her urged, but the lure of wealth suppressed it.

"Okay," she said, unsure about the plan. "How do I get to him?"

"Easy. Abner loves his Starbucks. You'll find him at the Los Gatos Boulevard Starbucks every morning around eight."

"And then what? I just walk up to him and introduce myself?"

Eddie threw up his hands. "Oh, come on. Of course not. Attract his attention somehow, or bump into him accidentally. Get him to notice you. That's it."

"That doesn't sound very practical. What if he ignores me?"

"Like I said, there's no way he's passing up on a beauty like you." He stroked his chin. "Though you're right — we need a bit more to get him hooked."

Eddie snapped his fingers. "Hey, you like Michael Connelly?"

Elsa replied with a blank stare.

"Okay, how about Ed McBain?"

"Never heard of either of them. Who are these people?"

He looked at her as if she had lost her mind. "You've never read any Connelly? No McBain?"

She shook her head. "I've read a lot of Colleen Hoover."

He frowned, then acted like he was going to throw up.

"Don't say anything about Colleen." She had to speak up. There was only so much of his nonsense she could tolerate.

Eddie held up his hands. "Okay. Okay. Just not my taste, alright? So Abner loves both of the authors I mentioned. Wednesdays and weekends he spends a long time at the Starbucks, book in hand, reading from cover to cover."

"So he's a nerd?"

Eddie shrugged. "Maybe he is, maybe he isn't. Who cares? The reason I told you this is so you could spot the book in his hand and tell him you're a fan too. That'll be a good icebreaker and could have you talking for hours, discussing books. The first step towards getting to his bedroom."

Elsa shuddered at the thought. "But I'd have nothing to discuss."

"Then read up."

"I ... I can't afford books right now."

"Then hit your local library. I'm sure they have several copies."

"Okay," she replied, though she was beginning to fear that this operation was a mistake.

Eddie was studying her now. It was as if she was in a job interview and he was evaluating her. Any moment now he would say she wasn't hired. Maybe she wasn't the right fit for this job. Or worse, he had figured out what she was up to. The thought worried her. There was a lot at stake here. She couldn't allow this opportunity to slip away. If there was even the slightest chance that this con would succeed, she had to grab it.

On the bright side, he hadn't leered at her like she was a piece of meat he would soon devour — something she was used to with other men. He was all professional, and it didn't seem like he would take advantage of her. She relaxed her grip on the pepper spray.

He sat down next to her and showed her his phone. On the screen was a man who seemed to be in his late twenties or early thirties, looking impressive in an elegant suit.

"That's him," Eddie said.

She took a closer look, unable to believe her luck. Somehow, in her head, she had conjured an image of Abner as a hairy, pot-bellied guy with a bald spot and a pug nose. The thought that she would have to seduce that monstrosity had repelled her. The real mark wasn't gorgeous, but he was presentable — a man she wouldn't mind chatting up if she met him on the street. A wave of relief washed through her. One less thing to worry about.

But who was she kidding? Appearance was only part of the equation. What if Abner turned out to be cruel and violent? A visually repulsive man who was loving and caring was still preferable to that. She wouldn't know what she was getting into until she spent some time with Abner.

"And he's single?" Elsa asked.

"Yeah. Doesn't surprise me. He's always either working or reading."

"Hmm." She considered that for a moment. "You're sure he's interested in women?"

Eddie chuckled. "Yes, I'm sure. It's not like he never entertains the beauties. It's just that, for a man his age and with his wealth, I'd have expected more."

"If he's so busy working all the time, why do you think he'll give me the time of day?"

"Trust me, he will."

Elsa was quiet as she mulled things over.

"Okay. So I spend a few days reading some Connellys and then bump into him at Starbucks. I pique his interest, we get to know each other. At some point he trusts me enough that I have a shot at stealing the money." She paused. "That could take forever. If it even happens."

Eddie shook his head. "You gotta be positive. This plan will work. Just try to speed it up as much as you can. I'd like to be rich by Christmas this year, not when I'm ready for a retirement home."

A smile slipped past Elsa's lips at the last comment. But it quickly turned into a frown as other concerns dawned on her. *How would she survive without any income until then?* As if he'd read her mind, Eddie reached into his pocket and produced a few Benjamins. He held out the bills to her.

"This should help tide you over until we hit the jackpot."

Elsa hesitated. It seemed strange to take money from him, even if it was only five hundred dollars. Well, not *only*, she thought. This cash could buy her a lot of groceries. Gas to get around. Maybe even contribute to rent.

"Think of it as an advance for the job," he said.

It was enough to convince her. She took it. "Thanks. But I'm still concerned. So much could go wrong."

Eddie gritted his teeth before looking at her. "You've never done a long con, have you?" He continued without waiting for a response. "Yes, things could go south. But you plan for it. Think it through in advance so you're ready for any hiccups and can take action accordingly. And if something unexpected happens, improvise. Think on your feet. Remember what's at stake — two million dollars." He said the last words slowly, emphasizing the amount. "Twenty with six zeros at the end."

Though he hadn't directly said it, the way he sneered at her and emphasized the twenty dollars, Elsa understood it was a dig at her and the dismal con she had pulled that morning. The barb stung, and she wanted to hit back hard, remind Eddie that it was five zeroes, not six. She might have botched her recent cons, but she wasn't dumb. But she held back, because insulting him now meant kissing this opportunity goodbye.

Before he could change his mind about their partnership, Elsa nodded her agreement and promised to keep him updated on her progress. Then she left, the walk back to her apartment filled with conflicting emotions — nervousness about what was to come, but also hope that things would turn for the better. She clung to that hope and, in spite of her whining belly, slept peacefully for the first time in days.

4

Elsa

Elsa waited across the street from the Starbucks, trying to keep her nerves in check. After a week of devouring Connelly novels, she was ready to approach Eric Abner. She had imagined every possible way this meeting could go wrong — ranging from *what if he isn't reading a Connelly this morning?* to *what if I trip and fall flat on my face, spilling scalding hot coffee on him in the process?* — so it was important she shoo those thoughts out of her mind and focus on the task ahead. What if he rejected her? Could she handle the disappointment of losing out on all that money?

She took a deep breath as she spotted Eric strolling towards the coffee shop, a paperback in hand. He seemed so calm, so relaxed, that she envied him. She crossed the street and entered the shop a few seconds after him. Getting in line behind him, she tried to glance at the book, hoping it was one she had read. But it was futile. She had considered bringing one of her own, but decided against it in the end. It could have looked too obvious and raised his suspicion.

Eric ordered a cappuccino, and when it was her turn, Elsa did the same, overcoming her hesitation at spending so much for coffee. A faint smile escaped her lips as she thought, *it's just a business expense*, grateful for the money Eddie had advanced her. She joined Eric as they waited for their orders, getting a glimpse of his book at last. By now her heart was galloping. She took another deep breath, adjusted her expression to one she considered to be her most pleasant and attractive, and took the plunge.

"A Connelly fan, I see," she said, looking him in the eye. His photos didn't do him justice. He looked a lot better in person than what his online presence had indicated.

He turned his attention to her, his face inscrutable, and for a moment she feared she had bombed. But then he beamed back at her as he held the book up.

"Yes. Are you a fan, too?"

She nodded and pointed to the book. "But I don't think I've read this one."

"It's a Bosch."

"Ah. I've only read the Renée Ballard and Lincoln Lawyer series."

"Those are good, but you should try Bosch. He's the best."

"I sure will."

Eric's order was up, and as he walked to retrieve it, Elsa relaxed a bit, savoring the brief break in her act. It had gone well so far, she thought, but could she drive it home? She heard her name just as Eric turned to face her with his coffee. She joined him at the counter and grabbed her cup, trying to steady her hands. As she turned away, he motioned towards an empty table, hesitating before he spoke.

"I hope I'm not being too forward here, but would you care to join me?"

He was smiling again, and his eyes showed his eagerness and how he hoped she would say yes. Elsa found it comforting, knowing that the first step was a success. Now if she could just keep it going well enough for him to request another date.

"I'd love to," she replied, trying not to sound too eager.

His smile grew wider, and his cheeks dimpled. The tingling sensation it produced within her took her by surprise. She speculated whether he was experiencing the same excitement, whether he was nervous too. Was there any part of her he considered so attractive that it was driving him crazy?

They walked to the table and settled into the chairs. Elsa took a sip of her coffee, waiting for him to make the first move. It was safer to let him lead lest she slip up and botch the entire operation.

Thankfully, Eric was all too keen to chat her up. They continued their discussion of Connelly, eventually moving on to other favorite books and movies. He was easy to talk to, and he knew exactly what to say to hold her interest. He told her he had grown up in San Jose and had been lucky enough to have a loving family and a good education. Elsa knew she would have to share her background at some point if they got intimate. She had considered making up stuff but had decided to play it safe and stick as close to the truth as possible.

She told him about growing up in Modesto and how her parents had been too broken to take care of her. She had scraped through school and college and had moved to San Jose first chance she got in search of a brighter future. She described her struggle finding and keeping jobs, but left out the bit about resorting to cons as her primary source of income. He listened intently throughout, and she could tell from the sparkle in his eyes that he was attracted to her. She only hoped her disastrous background wouldn't turn him away.

"So you're not working?" he asked when she took a breather.

"No. It's been difficult finding a job in this economy."

He remained silent for a while before replying.

"I might just have a position for you."

His reply took her aback.

"What's that?" she asked, intrigued.

"My buddy's receptionist quit last week, and he's scrambling for a replacement. I think you'll fit right in. If you're interested, that is."

He regarded her expectantly, unaware that regular employment was the least of her concerns. She had given up on that a long time ago, realizing it was not the thing for her. But turning him down could be detrimental.

"Oh, that would be wonderful." She was impressed by how well she delivered the line, as if Eric had thrown her a lifeline when she was close to drowning.

"Well, then. That's settled. Tomorrow morning, nine a.m. sharp. I'll text you the address. Once you share your digits with me, of course."

There was a twinkle in his eye as he said the last bit, and she convinced herself it was because he had found a way to get her number. She sincerely hoped he was interested in her romantically, or else it was all for nothing. If he was only offering her a job out of pity and he wasn't attracted to her, that would be a bummer.

Elsa gave him the number of the burner phone she had purchased specifically for this operation. She had assumed she would be using it to exchange romantic messages with Eric and plan their dates, but she hadn't expected to use it for employment leads.

They chatted a bit about this and that before parting ways. As she took the bus back home, she was more nervous than ever, unsure about how to prepare for the next morning. *Did she even have any professional clothes?* And how would she manage a regular nine-to-five job? How long would it take for Eric's friend to discover she was incompetent and fire her? *Had she messed up?* Perhaps it had been a mistake to share anything about her unemployment. But she was desperate to get her hands on Eric's fortune, and she would have to take her chances and hope for the best.

5

Elsa

Elsa was outside the doors of the office building in downtown San Jose at five minutes before nine the next morning. She had managed to dig out an old blazer and skirt set which she paired with a white blouse, hoping she appeared professional enough. Though she didn't care much about the job, it was important that she make a good first impression for Eric's sake.

She took a deep breath and stepped inside. The chart on one of the walls told her that Morris Securities was on the third floor. A short elevator ride later she entered the firm's lobby. A woman sat at the desk at the entrance, busy on the phone, prompting Elsa to wonder whether she was at the right place. Or, she thought with delight, maybe Eric's friend had already found a new receptionist. That would be a splendid development. She waited for the woman to end her call before approaching.

"You must be Elsa," the woman said before Elsa had a chance to speak.

"Yes, I am."

The woman stood up and extended her hand. "I'm Meredith. Welcome to Morris Securities. Brian told me you would be starting today. Brian — that's Brian Morris, our boss. Quite a relief for me, I can tell you that. I've been doing double duty helping out here since Anna quit. Anna — that's the previous receptionist."

Elsa shook her hand, taking in Meredith's words which came at a fast clip. Did the woman even breathe? She wondered why Anna had quit. *A better opportunity? Or something not right at Morris?* The latter possibility sent a shiver through her.

Meredith led her inside. The office was small, with four desks and chairs in the center, and a room on either side. The opposite wall was all glass and provided a view of downtown San Jose. Three of the desks were occupied, one man and two women. They all looked up as she entered and then went back to their computer screens. Meredith stopped at the unoccupied desk, and she motioned for Elsa to take a seat in the chair opposite. The next hour was spent going through new-hire paperwork and an overview of company policies.

Elsa learned that she would earn forty thousand dollars a year. In spite of her apathy for the job, a swirl of emotions rose inside her at the thought of earning an honest living again, though this salary wouldn't go far in the pricey Bay Area. What shook her, though, was the fact that her benefits included health insurance. That was a luxury worth working for.

Once the formalities were complete, Meredith introduced her to the others. The two women were Vicky and Sophia. The man was Roland. They were all pleasant. Then Meredith led her back to the front desk and explained the basics of the work. And just like that, at 11:00 a.m., Elsa began her job as a receptionist at Morris Securities. The next few hours were a blur, a time where she tamped down her nervousness and navigated the phone calls and the visitors quite well. By the time 5:00 p.m. rolled around and it was time to leave, she was exhausted.

After bidding goodbye to her coworkers and thanking Meredith for her help, Elsa exited the building. She was aching to rush home and relax, but to her surprise, Eric was waiting for her, sporting a goofy grin. Her real job was just starting, she realized with dismay. Flashing a smile of delight, she walked up to him. He took her hands in his, and this gesture sent a comforting tingle through her body.

"So how did it go?" he asked.

"It was great. Thank you."

"Don't thank me. I'm sure you'll do well. Brian is lucky to have someone like you."

She nodded. If he only knew the truth. The way he held her hands, the way he gazed at her, the fact that he was here waiting for her after her first day at work convinced her that he cared for her, that he was interested in her. It calmed her fears and gave her confidence that the operation was on track.

"I was hoping we could celebrate by grabbing some drinks, maybe dinner after. If you don't have any plans, that is," he said.

Home and relaxation would have to wait. This was her chance to take things to the next level, and there was only one appropriate response.

She smiled. "You read my mind. I'm starving."

The evening went by fast. They sat in a booth at Original Joe's, with Elsa downing a few margaritas and Eric running through his beers. By the time she had finished her massive entrée, she couldn't remember the last time she had felt so full. The conversation had been electric, and every time he grasped her hand or touched her, it was like he lit a fire. The duality of those embers concerned her. On the one hand, it was a comforting fire that warmed her soul; on the other hand, it scorched her, reminding her that she was deceiving this wonderful man. But there was no turning back now.

After dinner Eric walked her to her car. It was late and not a lot of people were around since it was a weeknight. Elsa was exhausted, and she contemplated how she would have the energy to get closer to him if she continued to work full-time. All she wanted to do now was get home and crash onto her bed. Maybe curl up with a book for a bit before drifting to sleep.

But he had other ideas. He moved in for a kiss. Their lips met, and all her exhaustion melted away, replaced with an electricity she hadn't anticipated. She kissed him back with an intense passion, which he reciprocated. When they parted after what seemed like an eternity, they both had glowing smiles.

Elsa wondered whether this was the moment when Eric would invite her back to his place — another significant advance towards her goal — but he turned out to be a perfect gentleman and eased her into her car and waved goodbye as she drove off. The smile didn't leave her face for a long time, and when she lay down in bed, sleep came in an instant, but not before she had relived the kiss over and over in her mind.

6

ELSA

The next morning Elsa woke up full of energy, moving around with a spring in her step, unable to get Eric out of her thoughts. She had to constantly remind herself that it was only a job, that he was only a means to an end and she shouldn't get swept away in dreams that would never materialize.

It was easy to forget about him once she was at work, for it was a busy day. Her coworkers made her feel comfortable, and the brief conversations she had with them throughout the day were enjoyable. Even her interactions with clients on the phone and with the in-person visitors infused joy inside her. She relished earning an honest living and being part of a team. Perhaps, she thought, there was a positive side to this unexpected job, though she hoped it wouldn't distract her from the end goal.

Soon after lunch Eddie texted her, asking for an update, and she responded with all the details. He was getting antsy, and she had to reassure him that things were going as planned, but it would be at least a few days before she would have a shot at the money.

Later, as she got ready to leave for the day, there was a flutter in her belly. *Would Eric be waiting for her outside?* He didn't disappoint. It was hard to tell who was happier when they laid eyes on each other. She walked up to him and kissed him without hesitation. Within minutes he swept her away for another delightful evening of drinks and dinner.

Elsa's heart grew heavy when they stepped out of the restaurant. As if sensing her discontent, Eric said, "Do you want to come over for coffee?"

"When?" she asked, breath laced with anticipation.

"Now," he replied.

This was it. The opportunity she had been waiting for. She couldn't say no. She didn't *want* to say no. It took all her self-control to not sound overeager. She paused a few seconds before replying.

"Yes. I would love to."

As soon as the words were out, the nervousness built up again. She knew what he meant by coffee. Was she ready for what was to follow? Her head told her she had no choice if she wanted the money. To her surprise, her heart agreed too, though the reasons were quite different.

Soon they were at his home in Los Gatos. A house so big it could accommodate ten of her apartments. Why a single guy like him needed so much space was a mystery. It looked grand from the outside, and it was even more impressive once she stepped inside. After Eric gave her a quick tour of the lower level, he pulled her close and kissed her. She didn't resist, and before long, coffee was forgotten as clothes were shed and more important pleasures were entertained. At some point he carried her upstairs to his bedroom, and they continued their encounter in bed. Later, she fell asleep in his arms, content.

When she awoke the next morning, it took her a while to figure out where she was. Seeing Eric beside her brought everything back, and she smiled. It wasn't just the bliss of their physical exertions that delighted her. She appreciated the comfortable mattress and the quality linen she lay on — nothing like the cheap stuff she was used to. How interesting that such mundane things could make such a difference.

Panic followed when she noticed the time. She tried to leap out of bed, but he held her back.

"Stay," he said, a sleep-infused request she found difficult to deny.

"I'll be late for work."

"On a Saturday?" A devilish grin adorned his face.

"Oh," she said as she fell back into his welcoming arms.

They lay like that for a while. Elsa enjoyed the calm and the warmth of Eric's body for a few minutes before her mind wandered, speculating about where his safe was, estimating how many such nights before she would get a crack at it.

"Breakfast?" he whispered into her ear.

"Mmmm ... sounds wonderful."

They put on robes, and she considered whether he always had an extra robe for the woman in his life, or if it was something he had purchased specially for her. He led her to the kitchen, directing her to sit at the breakfast nook. He cooked eggs and waffles, and she enjoyed every bit of it. She could get used to this pampering, she thought, before reality burst her bubble. This was a fleeting luxury. Her mission was to stab this man in the back by emptying his safe and disappearing from his life forever. The thought churned her stomach, and for a moment she thought she was going to lose her meal.

"You okay?" Eric asked.

"Yes." She nodded, forcing a smile and trying to stay calm lest he suspect something. There was something else that nagged her and added to her unease — the lurking fear that she would be found out, that this con would be yet another in her recent history of failures. It took quite an effort on her part to tamp down that insecurity.

Later, when she was alone in her apartment, she thought back to the previous evening and to the morning, and it brought a contentment she hadn't felt in a long time. Those were moments and memories that would always remain with her, no matter what happened in the future.

7

ELSA

Over the next few days they settled into a routine. Elsa spent most nights at Eric's, and on the following mornings she would shower and leave for work straight from his home. Work and the company of her colleagues continued to spark joy, something she couldn't say about any of the previous jobs she had held. It surprised her, because she'd heard that receptionist positions were boring and mundane. Perhaps it was interesting because it was novel to her? If she kept at it for a few years, would she hate it?

Her first paycheck in forever brought her to tears, and she appreciated being able to afford rent, however barely she scraped by. She savored that taste of success, something she had forgotten due to the rough patch she'd been going through. At least she wasn't going hungry anymore, and she was saving on groceries by filling up on dinner and breakfast courtesy of Eric.

Eddie continued pestering Elsa for updates, and sometimes the pressure stressed her out, but he backed off once she assured him she was making progress. She continued to read more Connelly novels in her spare time so that she would have more to discuss with Eric.

"This is a good one," he said one night, as she walked back to bed after brushing her teeth.

He was sitting up, paperback in hand. Her stomach knotted when she saw the title. *The Con Man*. There it was, the failure she had anticipated. He was onto her. But how? Her mind raced, trying to figure out where she had slipped up. Perhaps this was a coincidence? But what if it wasn't? She considered making a dash for it, calculating how many seconds it would take her to make it downstairs, how many to exit the house. Would she be able to get into her car in time? And where had she left the keys? If she scooted now, the head start could help her escape and avoid time in prison. To her dismay, she advanced towards the bed, as if in a trance. Her mind told her to scram, but her body had other ideas.

Think on your feet, Eddie had advised. *Improvise*. But she was helpless. She had lost her edge. If her string of failed cons hadn't convinced her already, this inaction certainly did. She was no longer cut out for this line of work. Perhaps a receptionist was the right career choice for her.

"Have you read any McBain?" Eric asked, pulling her out of her thoughts.

"No." She could barely get the word out.

"This is one of his early works. Interesting mystery about a con man. Though I feel his later novels were a lot better. You should try it sometime."

Through the fog of fear she sensed an irritation building inside her. He was toying with her, droning on casually about the story while driving a hot poker through her. She didn't give a damn about the book. All that mattered was whether she would get out of this predicament alive and well.

"I will," she replied, feeling like her fate was hanging in the balance.

"Con men always fascinate me. It's an art. All the planning that goes into the perfect con. And then the performance — playing the part just right to reel in the victim. Amazing stuff."

She settled into bed next to him, trying not to tremble. The more she watched him, the more she was convinced that this was a coincidence and he was clueless about her treachery. If he knew the truth, he would be raging, perhaps calling the cops, not having a normal conversation like this. When nothing untoward happened, she relaxed a bit, thankful that she hadn't attempted to escape. But she was unable to sleep due to the fear that had settled in her bones.

The terror held sway over her the next day as well, but relief came that night. They were lying in bed, spent after another session of passionate lovemaking, when Eric suddenly sat up.

"Come with me," he said.

She was concerned at first, wondering what he had in mind, but she had no choice but to comply. He took her hand and led her to his spacious walk-in closet. Her heart thudded with anticipation, her curiosity bubbling forth. He parted a bunch of elegant suits to reveal a door in the closet wall. He opened the door. Behind it was what she had been waiting for. The safe. *Finally*, she thought, straining to contain her excitement.

Elsa paid close attention as he entered the combination to open the safe. Her eyes grew wide and her jaw dropped when she saw the bundles of currency and the gold bars inside. She had imagined this several times, sure, but seeing it for real was something else.

"Wow." The word escaped her lips before she could rein it in.

"I don't know why, but I wanted to show you this. It's my emergency stash."

"Emergency stash? This looks like a thousand times my everything stash."

Eric chuckled.

"What kind of emergency?" she asked.

"I might sound paranoid, but it's doomsday preparation. You know, if there's a banking meltdown, for example. I'll have enough cash to survive. And if the dollar ever takes a dive, I've got good old-fashioned gold."

"Huh," she replied, not expecting this response. It was crazy. She wouldn't be surprised if he showed her an underground bunker next, stocked with canned food and gas masks.

"Can I ... can I touch it?" she asked.

"Touch what?" Mischief oozed out of his words and his face.

She realized how she sounded, considering they weren't wearing a shred of clothing between them.

"You sicko," she replied, laughing. "The cash. I don't think I've ever seen so much money in my life."

He tossed her a bundle, and when her fingers touched it, it had the feel of financial security. She sniffed it. It smelt of freedom. Soon this would all be hers. So close, yet it still seemed so far away and unachievable. *Would she be able to go through with the plan?*

She handed the bundle back to him.

"Isn't it dangerous keeping it here? Anyone could steal it. Or if, God forbid, there's a fire — this could all be gone. You would be better off leaving it in a bank locker."

Eric shook his head. "This safe is the finest out there. It's fireproof. The entire house could burn down and it would still be standing, unscathed. And as for burglars, the security is so great that no one can break into it. No one can drill into it. The only way in is with the combination."

It wasn't in her best interest to remind him, but she blurted it out anyway. "And you just shared the combination with me."

He stood up and approached her, placing one hand on her shoulder and gazing into her eyes. "Because I trust you, Elsa."

Her stomach lurched. It took quite an effort to keep her eyes locked with his and not let the guilt of betrayal force her to lower her eyes. He held up what looked like a jewelry box. She hadn't noticed where he got it or when he had picked it up, but it made her sick. Surely he wasn't going to get down on one knee and pop the question? She would be unable to handle that. No, that can't be it, she convinced herself. This would be too weird a situation to propose in. Both of them in his closet, naked. He opened the box to reveal a dazzling set of diamond earrings.

"I want you to have this," he said.

Elsa gasped. "They're beautiful. But I can't accept this."

"Please. You must."

His eyes were pleading, his tone insistent. She picked up the beauties and put them on, checking herself out in the mirror. Again, the incongruity of the scene jumped out at her — her standing there with nothing on but a pair of earrings worth several months' of her rent.

"Thank you," she said as she turned to him and kissed him, holding back the tears that threatened to emerge at any moment.

Eric locked the safe and they returned to bed. He was snoring within minutes, but try as she might, Elsa was untouched by sleep, the tumultuous debates in her head refusing to offer her any peace.

8

EDDIE

"Pizza?" Eddie asked Elsa who was seated in her usual spot on his couch, but looking unusually nervous.

She had shared the delightful news he had been waiting for. All the planning, all the fine execution, and now he stood on the verge of attaining the riches he had dreamed of. If he wanted, he could retire once this job was done.

Elsa accepted his offer and grabbed a slice — also unusual. Perhaps she was jittery about opening the safe and disappearing with Eric's money. It was one thing to string a guy along, intending to drain his wealth. Actually going forward with it was something different. Yet, he thought there was more to her nerves than met the eye.

"When do you see him next?" he asked.

"Tomorrow night."

"Then tomorrow it is."

It was only for a second, but he was certain he'd seen something in her eyes, an emotion that triggered warning bells in his brain.

"You sure you're up for it?"

"Yes." She nodded.

"I don't want to rush you, but you understand we have to move fast. It's been over two weeks since we started this operation, and now that you know the combination, it's best that you grab the money quick before something goes wrong."

"Yes, I understand."

Her tone wasn't convincing enough. His profession demanded that he excel at assessing people, and he was positive he was reading her right.

"You aren't in love with him, are you?"

The way her eyes darted up to meet his, the way the color rose in her cheeks, he knew he'd nailed it.

"I ... Don't worry, okay? None of that matters. What you need to know is that I'll be here with the money."

There was resolve in her eyes, and that calmed his fears a bit, though he still worried whether he had goofed by hiring her. She hadn't exactly dazzled with the locked car trick, but he'd been desperate to find a partner he could rely on, and one who was attractive and charming enough to seduce Abner. Anyway, it was too late to turn back now. She was all he had.

"Here you go," he said, tossing her a plastic bottle.

"What's this?"

"Put that in his water or beer or whatever he drinks at night. It'll knock him out for a few hours. That should give you enough time to empty his safe and run."

Elsa studied the bottle before turning her attention to Eddie. She didn't look convinced.

"It's just a sedative. It won't kill him or anything."

She nodded. "Okay."

Elsa finished her pizza and departed, leaving an unsettled Eddie in her wake. He fervently hoped she followed the plan and got him his money. *Women*, he thought. Even in his wildest dreams he couldn't have imagined that she would fall for Abner. But she had, and now it could derail his operation.

One more day. Only one more day and then he wouldn't need her anymore. As he had planned, he would be two million dollars richer and she could be on her way. If she raised a ruckus about not getting her share — well, he would just have to take care of her. No one would miss a lonely nobody like her. There was no way he was giving her a cent more than he already had.

9

Elsa

Elsa's hands were shaking by the time she got to her car. She had tried to stay calm in front of Eddie, but it was getting difficult to maintain control. He doubted her — she had seen it in his eyes. She had done pretty well until this evening, certain that he had no idea that him spotting her outside the 7-Eleven that morning was no coincidence. She had put on that show precisely so he would see her in action and consider her for the job. It wasn't her finest work, but it was the best she could do under the circumstances, given the short notice and the narrow window she'd had to capture his attention.

Desperate for money, her ears had perked up when she heard the chatter that a hustler named Eddie needed a partner for a lucrative con. She had considered approaching him and asking outright, but she feared he would turn her down like he had many others.

Not only was he ignorant of Elsa's scheme, he had no idea that he wouldn't be getting anything. Her plan all along was to abscond with the entire two million. But now her scheme was at risk, all because she had fallen in love with Eric and had been unable to hide it from Eddie. Would he be watching her closely? she pondered.

While the fear built up inside her, what troubled her most was the realization that her time with Eric was done. Tomorrow night she would meet him for the last time, and she wouldn't be spending it in his arms. She would drug him and rob him and leave his life forever. *Would his heart break at this betrayal?*

Without further thought she got into the car and drove, drove all the way to Eric's and knocked on his door, though it was late and he wasn't expecting her. A couple of minutes passed before he opened the door, and she spent that time in emotional turmoil, as if she had already lost him. As if she would never see him again.

"Elsa? Is everything okay?" he asked, the initial shock of seeing her on his doorstep turning to concern.

"Yes. I just ... I'm sorry for showing up like this."

"I'm delighted to see you, but I'm a bit miffed as well. Carella was about to nab the killer."

"Carella?"

"Oh, right. You haven't read any McBain yet."

"You were reading?"

"Yes. It helps me sleep when you aren't around," he replied with a smile.

"It's just that I missed you. I know we're meeting tomorrow, but I couldn't wait."

She rushed into his arms and kissed him. Every second counted, each one precious because there would be no more of these in her future. He shut the door and they hurried up to his bedroom, undressing each other as soon as they were inside. She savored every bit of him, from his lips to his body, as they made love that night. She traced her fingers over his face, his shoulders, his chest ... committing his form to memory, for these memories were all she would have of him.

Later, once Eric was asleep, she watched him. He genuinely cared about her, she was sure of it. One of those rare men who saw her as a real woman, an equal, with opinions and desires. Not just a beautiful plaything who satisfied his urges. A couple of nights ago he had asked if she had thought about her career, whether there was a field she was interested in. She could get a degree and move up from the receptionist job. She had never considered that option before, just assuming her life would be spent conning people.

The next day she had pondered over his question, about what she wanted. Her mind had drawn a blank. But did it matter? Tomorrow night she would betray Eric and empty his safe. Betray the only man who loved and respected her. The thought broke her heart, and as the sobs came in spite of her effort to suppress them, she was thankful that he wasn't awake to hear her. Closing her eyes, she tried to slip into that peaceful state, but it was futile. She passed the entire night tossing and turning, her conscience, her love for Eric battling her practical side.

The fact was, people like her didn't have a choice. She needed the money, and here was an opportunity she couldn't afford to miss. Not after everything she had been through. Sure, she now had what seemed to be a steady job and an income, but the financial struggle persisted. Eric's fortune, on the other hand, could transform her life. She could argue that he loved her, and she, him. That she didn't need to steal, that she could let the relationship continue. If she were lucky, some day they would get married and she would want for nothing.

But she couldn't base their relationship on a lie. If things got more serious between them, she would be compelled to confess. And where would that leave her? Eric was bound to be furious. He would cast her aside without a thought. Might even get her arrested out of spite, though she was yet to commit a crime. It would be so easy for a man in his position to get her busted on trumped-up charges. She couldn't take that chance. And if she tried to take what seemed to be the easy way out by not telling Eric, Eddie would make her life miserable.

The next morning, once Eric had left for work, she took a leisurely shower and ate a big breakfast though she was too nervous to enjoy it. It was the first time he had left her like this, but he had an early investor meeting to get to. Alone in that house, she imagined one last time what it would be like to be Mrs. Abner. Or perhaps Mrs. Gardner-Abner. To enjoy this luxury permanently instead of in limited segments like she did now.

She considered going to work as usual, returning later that evening and drugging Eric as planned, but she couldn't see herself doing that. There was no need for it now that she had the home to herself. She could take the money and leave right away. Better to get the job done before she had a chance to change her mind. It would also give her a head start on Eddie.

Elsa walked over to the safe, nervous that Eric might have come to his senses and changed the combination. To her relief, it unlocked without a hitch. She emptied the contents into a duffel bag she found in the closet. Then she hauled the bag to her car and drove away, steeling herself for the long drive to Mexico, fervently hoping she would make it without incident.

But first, she had work to do. The first stop was at her apartment to pick up her important stuff. Then she headed to Eddie's apartment. Scanning the neighborhood, she confirmed that his car was not present. She took a thousand dollars from her new-found wealth, walked over to his door, and slipped the money under it. While she was comfortable reneging on their deal, she believed she at least owed him something for the advance he had given her earlier. He didn't have to do that, but he had.

Elsa felt powerful for the first time in forever. Before today, there was no way she could have parted with this kind of money. But now she was walking away from it without a second thought. It was quite a heady feeling.

Her euphoria evaporated as soon as she turned onto the walkway leading to her car. Standing there, leaning on her Civic with a grim stare, was Eddie. Her head swam. Though she was outdoors, she could feel walls closing in on her, making it difficult to breathe. It took her right back to that night in Eric's bedroom, when she feared she had been discovered, except this was a hundred times worse.

Had Eddie been following her around? Is that why he hadn't been home? If he'd been watching her, then he must know that she had already stolen the treasure. It figured, considering how she had suspected that he was on to her the previous evening. She kicked herself for her carelessness, for not watching her back, for risking everything by coming here. Her brain implored her to run, but she was frozen in place.

"Where do you think you're going?" Eddie asked.

"I ..." Her heart hammered, threatening to burst out of her chest at any moment.

"What exactly have you been up to?"

"I ..."

He paused, studying her closely.

"Damn, you look like shit. Like you've seen a ghost. You still up for tonight?"

"Tonight?"

He shook his head, not caring to mask his irritation. "Abner. The money."

It took a few seconds for his words to sink in. But when they did, she took her first full breath in a while. Her heart eased up on its blistering pace. Once again, she had let her fears get the better of her. That's what failure and the resultant loss of confidence had done to her. *Eddie didn't know.* She was safe. For now.

She managed a smile and a nod. "Yes. Of course."

"What were you doing here?"

"Just meeting a friend."

The lies came easy now that she had exited panic mode, but he didn't look convinced.

"You didn't go in to work today?" he asked.

More probing. She wasn't out of the woods yet.

"I did. But I took a couple of hours off. My friend needed some help."

"I see." He moved closer to her and placed his hand on her shoulder. "Don't worry. You got this, girl. Just keep your cool and you'll do great tonight. See you after."

Elsa's body relaxed as Eddie walked away. Her breathing got back into rhythm. It was a close call, but she had survived. Something occurred to her as she watched him disappear around a curve. He would see the cash she had left him as soon as he entered his apartment. It would raise questions. She had better scram before he came looking for answers. Forcing her body into action, she hurried to her car, got in, and sped away, not daring to look back.

10

Elsa

Elsa lounged on the beach, watching the waves and enjoying her margarita as she had done for the past three days since arriving in Puerto Vallarta. A paperback copy of *The Con Man* rested on her belly, flanked by the coral bikini she had found in the hotel gift shop. She had been unable to resist swiping the book sitting on Eric's nightstand. Now that she had started reading it, she understood why he liked McBain so much. Definitely an author she wanted to read more of.

This was the life, she thought. Her stomach was full with the lavish breakfast. She was gradually forgetting what it was like to be constantly hungry, and the persistent worry about making rent every month. The rough patch in her life was a distant memory. She felt content, but just below the surface, there was guilt. Guilt for betraying Eric. *Was he heartbroken? Was he furious?*

Puerto Vallarta was nice, but she couldn't stay there forever. It was a popular enough destination that someone from her past life could easily spot her. This was only a rest stop. A place to celebrate her win before she flew out to a safer location. A permanent home.

"It wasn't hard to find you."

The voice sent chills down her entire body, reminding her that her run of bad luck hadn't ended. If anything it had continued with strength. She turned to look at the man relaxing on the lounge chair next to hers, a spot that until a few moments ago had been vacant. He had slipped in quietly.

"Eric ..." It was all she could muster as nausea pervaded her being.

"You thought you could dupe me?"

"I ..."

"Did you ever love me, or was it all a lie?"

She stared at him, unsure how to answer the question. His hurt tone was clear enough, but his dark sunglasses hid the entire picture. She wanted to see his eyes, to understand how he truly felt. Eventually, she decided to go with the truth. Things couldn't get any worse than they already were.

"It's true that I entered your life for the money. I caught your attention, pretended to love you so I could get access to your safe. But somewhere along the way, I did fall in love with you, Eric."

His jaw tightened. "Then why did you betray me?"

"I didn't have a choice. I didn't want our relationship to be based on a lie, but I thought if I confessed, you wouldn't believe me, and you would be so pissed that you would end it. Worse, you would turn me in and I'd rot in prison for a long time. So I took the money and ran."

"You could have just walked away. You could have spared that safe if you really loved me. You stole everything, Elsa. Everything I had."

His words were like a knife to her heart. But she wasn't sure she had the last part right.

"I know it was wrong, but you have so much more. This was only a small piece of it. For me that money is everything."

Eric laughed. "I don't blame you for believing that. How would you know, right?"

"Know what?"

"That cash, that gold — it was all I had. That, and your love."

"What are you saying? I don't understand."

"The media makes me out to be this real estate whiz, but the fact is, I'm awful at it. All this money I'm supposedly making, my high net worth, it's all fake. My business is bleeding. It's only propped up by new investors. It's kinda like a Ponzi scheme. The only thing of value I have is what you found in the safe. I'd been putting away a little regularly so I'd have something to escape with when everything collapsed. I already know the Feds have been sniffing around, and they're getting close."

"Oh." It was all Elsa could muster, unsure whether he was being truthful. If he was indeed speaking the truth, he was as much of a cheat as she was.

"So you've been defrauding investors?"

Eric winced.

"I never meant to. But project after project went off the rails, and I thought if I could just knock one out of the park I would be able to start paying back my investors. It's like those gambling addicts you hear about — they keep going deeper into debt hoping they'll hit the jackpot someday. But I was careful to take on only wealthy investors — people who could afford to lose that money."

"It's still wrong."

"I agree. But I don't think you're in a position to judge, are you?"

It was Elsa's turn to wince. He had a point — she made her living by duping innocent people, though not on the same scale as Eric. And her victims usually weren't rich. She was sure some of them couldn't afford to lose what she snatched from them. But in a dog-eat-dog world she had justified to herself that it was what she had to do to survive.

"How did you find me?"

He touched his ear lobe and grinned. A goofy grin she would have found adorable a few days ago, but now it grated. She frowned.

"Your earrings," he said.

Her hand went up to her ears, touching the spot where his gift would have been. She had locked them in the room safe before hitting the beach.

"I don't understand."

"The earrings I gave you — they have a tracker."

How dare he? a voice inside her raged once she understood what he was implying.

"You were spying on me? You gave me that *gift* so you could track me?"

"I'm sorry. I was taking a huge risk by sharing the combination with you, but this was the only way I could test your loyalty. I was sure you wouldn't go anywhere without those earrings, so at least I had backup in case you did take the money."

If Elsa had her pepper spray with her, she would have used it. That's how furious he had made her. Without her weapon of choice, she considered a kick in the nuts instead. But another voice inside her reminded her that she had no right to be so angry. She had conned him, and he was only trying to protect himself. She would have done the same if she had been in his position.

"I don't understand. Are you saying you knew I would take your money?"

Eric nodded. "It might sound silly, but I fell in love the moment I laid eyes on you that first morning. The only problem was, with the Feds breathing down my neck I couldn't let just anyone enter my life like this and get so close to me. So I had you checked out. I had to ensure you weren't an undercover agent trying to entrap me. That's when I learned who you were and why you had targeted me. By then I was in too deep."

The debate within her raged on. One voice hated him for not trusting her enough, for digging into her background. Despised him for duping her like this. The other voice reminded her that she had brought it upon herself by cheating him.

"Why didn't you stop me if you knew?"

"Because I'm stupid. Crazy in love. It was your beauty that attracted me at first, but, Elsa, you're so much more than that. In these few weeks that I've known you, I've seen you to be kind and loving and caring. In your presence I've felt a warmth that I've never experienced before. And, yeah, I know one could argue it was all part of your act, but I don't believe that. I hoped that if I showed you how much you meant to me, you would love me back and not steal from me. That, and the fact that you caught me off guard. I suspected you wouldn't make your move for another day or two."

Elsa's heart broke at this confession. If only she had confided in him.

A question crossed her mind — was his recklessness limited to matters of the heart, or did it extend to his work as well? If it did, that would explain a lot about his business failures. Something she would have to discuss with him at some point if there was the slightest chance of a future together.

"I do love you, Eric."

"I know."

He extended his hand to her. She hesitated before taking it, his warmth comforting her, making her realize how much she had missed his touch.

"If you knew where I was all this time, why did it take you so long to find me?"

"I had stuff to wrap up. Plus, I needed some time to think things over. The fact is, at first I hated your guts for what you did, but then I realized I loved you way more."

"I'm sorry. I made a mistake."

He waved her off. "It's okay."

"Is it, though? I flunked your test. Miserably." She recalled that moment in the closet together — *I trust you, Elsa*, he had said. A gentle nudge to do the right thing. One that she had ignored.

"You were desperate. I get it. But when I look at you now, I can see that your heart's in the right place. That's what matters the most."

They were silent for a bit before Elsa spoke.

"I'm worried Eddie will be looking for me."

Eric smiled.

"Well, everyone's looking for you."

"What do you mean?"

"To the world, you've gone missing. Morris checked up on you when you didn't show up for work. Meredith and the rest of the staff were all so worried, concerned about the friendly girl and awesome receptionist who suddenly vanished."

"Oh, I feel so bad for them."

"Don't. They'll get over it. And you don't need to worry about Eddie. I took care of him."

"Took care of him? How?"

"Since I needed to disappear anyway, thanks to the Feds, I made it look like there was foul play at my home. Anyone investigating will think I was attacked and I'm missing, most likely murdered. That should be the end of their case against me. And I left enough *evidence* to make it look like Eddie's behind it all."

A burst of laughter escaped Elsa before more rational thoughts took over. She had to stay safe from Eddie, but he didn't deserve this punishment. Implicating him for murder was a bit much.

As if sensing her concern, Eric said, "Don't feel sorry for him. I know you think he's just a harmless con man, but he has hurt plenty of people. I see this as payback."

"But he told me he wasn't into violence. No guns. No knives."

"Well, he lied. He tries to avoid it, sure, but he isn't afraid to use force where necessary."

Elsa was silent. Eddie's fate didn't sit right with her, but at least she could rest easy knowing he wouldn't pursue her.

"So you're Stacey Kowalski now?" Eric asked, changing the topic.

"Yes. It's an identity I'd got made a while back. How did you find out?"

"Some sleuthing at the front desk."

"I see. And what's your new name?"

"Mike Jones."

Elsa laughed again. As she did so she realized that the only person who had made her laugh like this in the last few years was Eric.

"That is so—"

"Plain?" he said before she could finish.

"Yes."

"Good. That's what I was going for. A man on the run doesn't want to stand out in any way."

"I guess I should have picked something less memorable."

Eric shrugged. "It's a beautiful name. Just like your original."

"If you were to pick one for me, what would you pick?"

He studied her for a bit before replying. "My first choice would be Emma, but that's another E ... Mary, perhaps? Yeah, Mary Jones."

Elsa blushed at his choice of last name. Had he selected it because it was a common one, or was he hinting that someday they would be married and she would take his last name? Her mind wandered to that night in his closet, the moment when she thought he was going to propose. Was that even a possibility now, after her betrayal? Would she accept if he asked her? A part of her still couldn't stomach the fact that he had lied to her and cheated others.

"So what next?" she asked, nervous about Eric's plans and what it meant for her.

"I'd like to give it a shot. Us, I mean."

A wave of relief passed through Elsa. While she had sensed that he wouldn't hurt her in any way for her treachery, hearing it from him helped. She would have the money and a life with Eric.

"Are you sure about this?" she asked. "I mean, we've both lied to each other. Our relationship is based on falsehoods. Any strong relationship needs trust. Do we have that?"

Eric gave it some thought. "You're right. But now that we've come clean, we can start over. Build trust slowly, over time. I love you too much to not give it a shot."

His sunglasses were off now, and his eyes pleaded sincerity. Perhaps he really had no ill intentions here. But could she rely on her own ability to read this man? She had fallen for his tricks before. How could she be certain he wasn't lying again?

"It seems you need some time to think it over," he said.

Elsa nodded. She was getting sick of this turmoil within her, this flip-flop of emotions.

"I'm going to go for a swim. Give you some space. This has been a lot for you to take in."

As she watched him go, she had the urge to pull him back, as if she was losing him again. She leaned back on the chair and closed her eyes. It helped, because all she witnessed were the blissful moments she had spent with Eric. *It will work,* the voice inside convinced her.

When she opened her eyes, she scanned the water for him, worried at first when she didn't spot him. Then he emerged from the water, reminding her how, years ago, she had gaped at the screen in excitement as the sculpted figure of James Bond did the same, albeit in tiny trunks. Eric was no Bond, his trunks leaving everything to the imagination, and his body hinting at only a passing acquaintance with the gym. Yet, she was just as excited to see him. There was something irresistible about him that she had never been able to explain.

He doesn't love you. Doubt crept in again. What if this was all a ruse? What if he was aching for revenge, furious that she had dared betray him? *He's after the money.* He didn't know where she had stashed it. He needed her help to get it, and what better way to do that than to convince her he loved her? It was a possibility. He had conned her before, and he could be doing it again right now. What would he do once he had what he wanted? Would he just disappear, or would he kill her? He was ruthless enough to implicate Eddie for murder. It wouldn't surprise her if he got back at her by hurting her. The thought made her nauseous.

A few more steps and Eric would be beside her again. Elsa noticed his captivating smile, those dimpled cheeks. Again, she tried to focus on the positive, convincing herself that her bad luck phase was over. That she was now entering the golden period of her life. That she wouldn't have to worry about food or rent anymore. That she would build a great life with this man. That he would love her forever, and he would never, ever, hurt her.

She squeezed his hand tight and pulled him down for a kiss, hoping for her sake that she was right.

THANK YOU!

Dear reader,

Thank you for reading *The Con*! If you enjoyed this story, please post a review on your favorite platforms. Reviews help more readers find me and my books, so a positive review can be very helpful and is immensely appreciated.

◈

To learn more about me and my work, visit https://www.vineetvermaauthor.com. You can also sign up for my newsletter there to receive the latest updates about my writing, get book recommendations, and follow links to cool book promos. If you prefer social media, you can follow me here:

Facebook: @VineetVermaAuthor
Instagram: @vineetvermaauthor
X: @VineetvAuthor

OTHER TITLES BY VINEET VERMA

"A twist here and a turn there make this book one that is hard to put down!"

Bestselling author Daniel Geraldi has it all — a beautiful wife, loving kids, and a thriving career. At least he thinks he does until he faces betrayal of the worst kind. Still reeling from the shock, he's tempted into a relationship with a flirtatious fan. Soon his family is the target of some disturbing incidents and he suspects that this fan, Penelope, is responsible. As he investigates, tragedy strikes and things take a turn for the worse. Can he protect himself and his family?

https://books2read.com/u/mB159M

"Barefoot in the Parking Lot is a suspenseful mystery with a cast of characters readers will love to hate."
When the hotshot CEO of a famed AI company and tech powerhouse is found dead, detectives Angela White and Paul Conley are called in to investigate. The deeper they wade into the evidence, the longer the suspect list grows.

They soon come face-to-face with the dark and sordid world that lies just under Silicon Valley's polished and pristine exterior. From jealous ex-lovers to rival tech giants, Jay has created powerful enemies, all of whom would be happy to see him dead--and all of whom have solid alibis. White and Conley hit dead end after dead end. And when blackmail schemes and copycat murders come into play, finding the killer becomes increasingly more urgent. Can they catch a break, or will a murderer go free in Silicon Valley?

books2read.com/u/3JXAWA

"Devious Minds is a must-read for fans of short fiction looking for stories with dark themes, shocking twists, and insights into the criminal mind."

When you hear the word "criminal", what comes to mind? A cold-blooded killer? A professional burglar? Perhaps someone peddling drugs? People who indulge in illegal activities everyday. But sometimes it's just regular Joes like you and me. Men and women who do honest work, staying within the limits of the law, until one day they can't take it anymore and they commit a crime. But what is it that makes them crack? Was there something devious always lurking under the surface, waiting to emerge?

Devious Minds is a collection of crime stories, including police procedurals, psychological thrillers, and more that will suck you into a world of mystery and suspense. Fasten your seat belt and enjoy the ride!

https://books2read.com/u/47WjdA

ABOUT THE AUTHOR

Vineet is a tech professional by day and has been a lifelong fan of mysteries, be it in books or on screen. He enjoys writing and creating a world of suspense that leaves his readers guessing until the end. With his debut novel, *Barefoot in the Parking Lot*, and the follow up short story, *The Stick*, he fulfilled his dream of becoming a published author. He lives in San Jose, California with his wife and twin boys and hopes to keep plumbing the depths of his twisted mind to write for years to come.

www.ingramcontent.com/pod-product-compliance
Lightning Source LLC
LaVergne TN
LVHW092057060526
838201LV00047B/1439